The Dangerous
Small Red Car

The Dangerous Small Red Car

Mary Mwangangi

PUBLISHERS LTD

The Dangerous small red car
First Published in 2011 by
Focus Publishers Ltd
P O Box 28176
Nairobi

© Mary Mwangangi 2011

Illustrations
Victor Obwocha

Cover Design: Planet Creative/Celestina Kamene

ISBN: 9789966011602

Printed by English Press Ltd
Enterprise Road, Industrial Area
P O Box 30127
Nairobi

Chapter 1

Eleven-year-old Kimosop and his classmates Kadzo, Taabu and Tobiko were very happy as they went home. They were looking forward to a good rest over the weekend after a busy five days in school. They talked and laughed aloud as they shared the day's experiences at school. They also made plans for the weekend as they playfully walked along the familiar paths towards their homes.

A short while later they heard a vehicle approaching. They looked behind and noted that it was one of the lorries that carried sand from one of the river beds near their school. It was moving at a slow speed.

"We are going to get a free ride," said Kimosop.

"It won't stop for you," said Kadzo.

"You will see," said Kimosop and before they could discuss the issue any further Kimosop jumped and held on to the back of the lorry as it went past them. Tobiko followed suit. The two girls watched in awe as the lorry disappeared out of sight with the two boys hanging gleefully at the back.

★★★

Kimosop jumped and held on to the back of the lorry as it went past them. Tobiko followed suit.

The following day Kadzo and Taabu were surprised to find themselves being interrogated by the Police on the whereabouts of Kimosop and Tobiko. The two children had not arrived at home as expected. At first Kadzo and Taabu did not want to disclose how they had parted with their classmates but after a lot of questioning by the police officers they confessed what had happened.

Thereafter the police officers questioned all the lorry drivers who harvested sand on that route but none of them wanted to be involved with the Police as they were aware that their activities of sand harvesting were illegal and detrimental to the environment. They feared that they could be arrested. The police officers also questioned the driver of the lorry that Kimosop and Tobiko had jumped onto but he denied having driven on that road on the day in question.

The truth was that the lorry driver was lying. He had noted Kimosop and Tobiko as they jumped onto his lorry but did not stop to warn them against such dangerous behaviour because he had an evil plan for them. After driving for sometime, he turned left into a narrow track. His aim was to scare Kimosop and Tobiko so that they could jump out of the lorry. They did just that. None of them was hurt hence they walked away amused and pleased with the distance they had covered. The lorry driver also drove away towards the forest pleased with himself because he had also accomplished his mission. He knew that Kimosop and Tobiko had jumped out of the frying pot into the fire.

As soon as the lorry disappeared the two boys started to walk along the road so as to catch a bus or a *Matatu*. They waited and waited but there was no Matatu or any vehicle on the road. There were no people on the road either. It was now getting dark. Tobiko recalled that his mother had always advised him to stay away from poorly lit and isolated areas hence he became scared and started to cry but Kimosop assured him that they would be safe. A short while later Kimosop said;

"Look, I can see some car lights. May be it is a Matatu. But even if it is not a Matatu we shall stop it and ask for a ride."

"But the teacher told us not to talk to strangers or take a ride from people we do not know. What if we get into trouble?" Tobiko asked his friend.

"It is getting late and there is no time to reason. It is better to be inside a vehicle than out in the dark," Kimosop reasoned.

Kimosop waved down the vehicle. It stopped. It was a small red car with two passengers, a man and a woman.

"Hello children, it is getting late and you should not be on the road at this time. How far are you going?" the lady asked sweetly.

"We got late from school. Our home is just about half a kilometre from here. Could you please give us a ride? We have some money. We can pay for the ride."

"No problem, jump in. And you don't have to worry about payment. This is a private car and we are going the same direction," the lady told them.

Kimosop and Tobiko were very happy. At least they would not get home very late and would not get into trouble. In fact they expected they would get home before Kadzo and Taabu and they would boast to them how they had managed to get home before them.

Kimosop and Tobiko had used that road so often that they knew all the landmarks so when they got in the vicinity of their home Kimosop shouted to the driver; "We have arrived. Thank you very much. Please stop." But the driver continued as if he had not heard him.

"Hey! You have passed the road to our home. Please don't go any further," Kimosop shouted at the top of his voice. However the driver continued driving.

"Madam," Kimosop said to the lady. "Please ask him to stop. We don't even know how we will get home from here," but the lady did not respond either. She did not even look at them.

Kimosop and Tobiko held each other and started to sob but the car driver and the lady did not bother with them. They just continued to drive. The two children cried until they both slept.

CHAPTER 2

THE next morning Kimosop and Tobiko woke up and found themselves sleeping on mats in a strange house.

"Where are we," Kimosop asked Tobiko.

"I don't know. I told you we should not take a ride from strangers but you did not pay attention. Now see," said Tobiko.

"See what? I did not force you to get into the car. You could have refused and walked home," Kimosop retorted.

As the two boys were arguing two other children entered the room. One of them was Masengo from their school. Masengo was one of the most admired boys in their school because he was always concerned with the school's environment. He usually collected litter within the school's compound while others were busy playing and often encouraged them to join him. As a result the school compound was so clean that the headmaster did not have to employ people to do the job. This earned Masengo special recognition during the school's parents' day.

On another occasion Masengo had used his father's camera to secretly take a photograph of a butcher who often bought goats and carried them to his butchery on his bicycle. Masengo always felt that it was not right so he took the picture to one of his teachers who also took it to the Police. Masengo and all the other children were surprised to learn that carrying a goat on a bicycle was a crime as it was regarded as cruelty to animals. The butcher was arrested and fined five thousand shillings.

A few weeks later Masengo failed to turn up in school. His parents said Masengo had left home at seven o'clock as usual and were surprised to hear that he was not at school. The whole neighbourhood looked for Masengo but could not find him. Most people, including the Police, suspected that it was the butcher who had made an evil plan against Masengo but the Police could not find evidence to connect the butcher with Masengo's disappearance. It was as if Masengo had vanished into thin air. So when Kimosop and Tobiko saw Masengo they cried out in disbelief.

"Masengo, we thought you were dead!"

"Shhh," responded Masengo. "Did you come here in a small red car?"

"Yes," they both responded.

"Same with me. I asked for a ride from a man and a woman in a small red car. They were so generous that they even offered me some sweets. I think the sweets were drugged because I ate one and instantly felt drowsy and then slept. When I woke up I found myself here."

"Masengo, we thought you were dead!"

Turning to the other boy he said; "This is Kones. He was brought here a month ago in the same car."

"My mother must be dead by now," Kones said. "I am her only child and have now vanished. They found me on my way to the local dispensary and stopped to give me a ride. I thought they were very considerate especially when they said they would wait for me to get medication and then take me home. The lady even paid for my treatment. I gave them direction to our house and they told me to sleep and that they would wake me up when we got to the general area so that I can point out our house. I believed them but when I woke up I found myself here. I am sure my mother did not bother to check at the dispensary since I had not told her that I would be going there."

"But our teacher told us to always tell our parents or someone where we are going. Did you not tell anybody that you are going to the dispensary?" asked Tobiko who could now recall most of the things they had been taught during road safety lessons.

"Yes, we were but I did not imagine it could happen to me. It is too late now. It can not help me. No wonder it is said that experience is the best teacher."

"Do they just lock you in here the whole day?" Kimosop inquired.

"No, we walk to a place where they are planning to put up another house and wait for a lorry that delivers sand, stone and ballast. Then we remove them and arrange them as directed.

"And why don't you run away if you work in the open field?"

"You can't. There is always someone watching us." Before they could carry out any further conversation an ugly tall hefty man entered the room. He was carrying a tray with four cups of porridge. They all kept quiet.

"Good morning boys. I hope you had a good night's sleep. Here is some nice hot porridge for you. It will make you warm and strong for the day's work. Masengo and Kones, have you narrated to your new friends how you spend the day?"

"Yes," they both replied in low tones.

As they talked Masengo and Kones grabbed their cups of porridge and started to gulp in a hurry. Kimosop and Tobiko could not understand how they could start drinking the porridge so fast.

"I will see you in a minute," said the hefty man and then left.

As soon as he left Masengo said;

"Please swallow your porridge as quickly as you can because he will be back in a few minutes to walk with us to the building site whether you have drunk it or not. It is better to have something in your tummy or else the day can be rough."

"Who is he?" asked Kimosop.

"His name is Mbaya. He guards us so that we don't escape and he can be evil," Masengo answered.

On hearing this Kimosop and Tobiko joined the others and gulped their porridge. A few minutes later Mbaya came for the boys.

"Let's go," he said.

"Go to where? I want to go home," said Kimosop.

"Why do you ask that? Have your friends not told you what they do the whole day? You are going to wait for some building materials and remove them from a lorry. There is no pay for this work. Your pay is the food you will eat. If you don't work as expected you will not eat. I shall be watching you as you work," said Mbaya and then went on to say;

"If you try to run away, I will blow my whistle and these dogs will run after you. Once they get hold of you they will drag you back. They will also bite you all over." He said this while pointing to the four ugly dogs which had accompanied him.

"Thereafter you will have to continue working but will not eat anything for the next three days. However, if by any chance you manage to escape from the dogs your chances of survival will not be any better because you will definitely be eaten by a lion. There are many lions around here. Okay let's go."

Kimosop and Tobiko started to weep while Masengo and Kones remained quiet. The two boys had cried enough. The four dogs wagged their tails as if to welcome Kimosop and Tobiko.

"There comes the lorry," said Masengo.

Kiomsop and Tobiko looked up and to their surprise they noted that it was the same lorry they had climbed onto. The lorry driver looked at them and waved at them to begin working. The four boys went on to remove the stones and arranged them as directed by Mbaya. They worked until lunch time. They then took an half hour break during which they were given a cup of black coffee and five slices of bread each.

The two boys had cried enough.

"Please put some butter on the bread. I am not used to eating it like this," said Kimosop.

"This is not a hotel. Eat it or leave it for my dogs can make better use of it," said Mbaya. He then moved forward to take Kimosop's bread.

"I am sorry. I will eat it the way it is. Please don't take it away. I am very hungry," Kimosop pleaded.

He then started eating his bread while the others just watched the drama quietly.

A second later Kimosop sipped his coffee. Once again he started complaining

"This coffee has no sugar. Please add some milk and sugar. It tastes awful.

"You are just a spoilt child. Take your coffee or leave it. There is no milk or sugar around here. In any case sugar is no good for your health. Haven't you ever heard of a disease called diabetes?"

"I am not used to taking coffee like this," Kimosop quipped.

"Then bring it. My dogs can enjoy it. They are not spoilt like you. They eat and drink anything. And that includes people like you."

On hearing this Kimosop started taking his coffee. However, before he could eat his fifth slice Mbaya started collecting the utensils.

"I am not finished," Kimosop screamed.

"Who cares? Time is up. You spent your precious time complaining about butter and sugar. Did you not know that you have only one mouth and had to use the same mouth for eating?" said Mbaya as he took away Kimosop's last slice of bread and threw it to the dogs. The dogs ran and started fighting over it as Kimosop watched in disbelief.

The boys worked until six o'clock in the evening. Mbaya inspected their work as they anxiously watched and then said;

"Good job. Let us go home now."

"That is not home for us," Kimosop retorted,

"You have a big mouth and it could cost you your dinner."

Kimosop was not used to hard work and was already starving, so he kept quiet.

THREE weeks later Kimosop and his collegues were still off-loading stones and other building materials. Meanwhile all the parents, teachers, the Police, and everybody had searched for them everywhere in vain. Some parents had even started accompanying their children as they walked to and from school while others stood guard as their children played outside.

Many police officers visited schools to educate children about being safe on the road. They told the children to follow safe routes to school and to avoid short cuts and isolated areas. Kadzo and Taabu could remember that on the day Kimosop and Tobiko had disappeared they had followed a short cut and had even played with millipedes and butterflies. The Police and parents had searched every bush and cave in that area in vain.

The Police also advised the children that it was always safer to walk with a friend or in a group rather than alone. Kadzo recalled that on the day Kimosop and Tobiko disappeared they were walking in a group of four before they separated. This was not a good idea. They should have continued their journey home as a group.

Some parents stood guard as their children played outside.

She always felt guilty about the disappearance of Kimosop and Tobiko as she was the oldest in the group.

The children also learnt many other things from the Police. They were told to always identify places they can run to in case of danger and to report any suspicious activities, or anything that does not seem right.

"Report to whom?" Achieng asked during one of the lectures.

"You should report to your teacher or parents or even the Police," one of the police officers answered.

"I am scared of the Police, and I don't like them," said Achieng.

"Don't. The Police are employed to protect you from danger. Any time you sense danger you should run to the Police. Is that clear?"

"Yes sir," the children answered in unison as most of them stared at Kadogo whose mother was a police woman. Kadogo was not amused by Achieng's comment. After all Achieng was one of her best friends who often accompanied her to their house. They often tried on her mother's police cap whenever the mother was away. How could she make such a comment?

"What is it young girl?" The Policeman asked Kadogo on noticing that she was not happy.

"Her mother is a policewoman," another child said.

"Sorry Kadogo, I did not mean your mother. She is very nice. I meant the others," said Achieng who was now sorry for blurting out words without thinking.

"That is even better," said the policeman. "I also have children and now you can see that one of your schoolmate's mother is a police officer. Policemen and women are also parents like your parents. You should not be scared of them."

"Yes sir," the children said as they clapped. This made Kadogo smile as Achieng went and hugged her.

In the meantime the occupants of the red car continued to patrol the roads for more victims but did not get any as all the children and their parents were on alert. At the same time Kimosop and the others continued to toil in the forest.

One day, as the four children were working, Tobiko became stressed and hit one of the shovels against a tree. It was an old shovel hence it split into two. This annoyed Mbaya who started to yell at Tobiko calling him a lazy and good for nothing fellow. The dogs surrounded Tobiko as if waiting for a command to chew him up. Tobiko started to scream and this annoyed Mbaya even more because he did not want anyone to know about the children. He continued to lecture Tobiko.

On noticing that the dogs and Mbaya were all concentrating on Tobiko, Kimosop escaped towards the bush and ran as fast as his legs could carry him. There was no road or foot paths to follow. He just ran and avoided the bushes and trees as best as he could. Before long he tripped and fell down but this did not discourage him. He got up and continued running. For him this was a matter of life and death.

After Mbaya was finished with scolding Tobiko he turned round and immediately noticed that Kimosop was nowhere to be seen.

"Where is Kimosop?' he roared.

The boys looked up in surprise as they too had not seen Kimosop disappear.

"Where is he?" he ranted as he whipped each of them with a leather strap. The boys held on to each other and started to cry.

"We don't know. We thought he was still here," the boys responded truthfully in tears.

"Quick. Go back to the house. I have to lock you up and go to find him. I will teach him a lesson."

The boys ran to the house with the dogs closely following them. After locking them up Mbaya and his dogs went to look for Kimosop. The dogs led the way as they had picked Kimosop's scent.

By this time Kimosop had covered a lot of ground but Mbaya and the dogs who knew the forest better were catching up with him. Kimosop could now hear the dogs barking close by. He was very scared. He thus decided to hide in a thick bush and held his breath. Three of the dogs passed where Kimosop was hiding as Mbaya followed them running.

"Get him and chew him up! That is your meal for the day," Mbaya screamed as he too ran behind the dogs. Kimosop remained motionless until the dogs ran out of sight.

He was about to breath a sigh of relief when the fourth dog appeared. He had not noticed that only three of the four dogs had ran past him. The dog which Mbaya always referred to as Papa was the youngest. It ran past close to where Kimosop was hiding but before Kimosop could thank his God for the narrow escape the dog came back. It stopped in front of the bush where Kimosop was hiding and started to sniff around. Then their eyes met. Kimosop knew that his end had come. The dogs would make a meal out of him as Mbaya had promised them. He was scared to death. Kimosop went on his knees and started pleading with the dog.

He was very scared. He thus decided to hide in a thick bush and held his breath.

"Papa, I know you can hear me even though you are a dog. Please have mercy on me. We were taught that a dog is a man's best friend. Be my friend and save me from Mbaya. I know you don't like him either. He does not take care of you as he should. He should be buying you some dog food and bones but instead he only feeds you on bread and ugali. Remember how you had to fight over my slice of bread? Dear God please talk to this dog," Kimosop pleaded with a murmur.

To Kimosop's surprise Papa did not bark so as to alert Mbaya and the other dogs that he was there. He just stared at Kimosop as he talked and talked. Suddenly Kimosop heard Mbaya coming back to look for the dog. Papa. Where are you? Have you found him?" he asked. He came up to where Papa was but before he saw Kimosop the dog started running in the direction the other dogs had gone. Mbaya looked around but did not see Kimosop who had squeezed himself behind the bush. Papa continued barking as he followed the others.

"Run and find him," Mbaya screamed as he followed the dogs.

"Thank you God," Kimosop said as he looked up to the sky. Kimosop did not want to move out of his hiding place lest Mbaya came back the same direction.

He was right. A few minutes later Mbaya came back accompanied by the dogs. They run past him without stopping. Papa lagged behind and stared at Kimosop again. He wagged his tail and ran after the others.

Chapter 4

As soon as Kimosop was sure that Mbaya and the dogs were out of sight he started running faster than before. He ran until his legs could no longer hold his weight. It was also getting late and he was scared of the animals Mbaya had told them about. He decided to rest for a short while since he could not go any further even if he wanted to. Every part of his body hurt. He was also hungry and for a moment he missed Mbaya's sugarless tea and bread without butter. But he would not go back no matter how hard things became.

"I must get home so that the others can be saved. It is better for one of us to be out of that place than for all of us to be under Mbaya's watch," he told himself.

After about thirty minutes Kimosop decided to get up and start walking. Suddenly he heard something move close to where he was. He was sure it was an animal. Now he would be eaten alive as Mbaya had said. He looked anxiously towards the direction he had heard the sound. Then he saw it. It was a brown and white animal with small horns. It also looked at Kimosop. Fortunately Kimosop had grown in the countryside so he could tell the difference between a wild animal and a domestic animal. This was a domestic animal, a goat. Kimosop was so happy. At least he could talk to the shepherd who was looking after the goats. He would probably be kind enough to take him to his home, give him some tea with bread and butter and help him get home. But Kimosop did not want to show himself before he saw who was with the animals so he just sat still. To his surprise the young boy who was in charge of the animals did not come from the direction he was looking at. He came from behind him. Kimosop wanted to scream.

"Shhh. Are you running away from Mbaya?" the boy asked him.

"Yes, please help me," Kimosop begged.

"I am in a no better position than you are. I came here in a small red car with a man and a woman. They found me playing with a ball with my friends in a field. There was no adult close by. They stopped as if to check whether their car had a puncture. At that time our ball went to the direction of their car. I ran to get it. I was also curious to know why the car had stopped. By the time I got there the woman had picked the ball. She stretched her hand as if to hand it over. Before I took it she got hold of me, then the driver came out, got hold of me and pushed me into the back seat. I cried and cried until I slept. When I woke up I found myself in the same house I think you have ran away from."

Kimosop was quiet for once since he was keen to hear about the boy's story. The boy continued.

"One day I ran away as we were working in the field with another boy named Kones but before I could get any far the dogs caught up with me. The dogs almost killed me. They bit me all over. Thereafter I was moved to this place. There are six of us. We take care of cows, goats and pigs. Some of the boys who live with me told me they were removed from other shelters within the forest."

"Why don't you run away? At the moment you are all by yourself."

"I am not alone. There is always someone watching us. We never know in which direction he is patrolling. Moreover, if they catch you after you try to escape they really beat you. If you try it the second time they kill you immediately after they get hold of you. So we would rather lie low in the hope that one day we will be found alive. I wish you all the best. If you manage to get home, don't forget us. Just tell them to search the forest thoroughly. There are many of us around this place." Kimosop was about to run when he heard a whistle blow.

"He is looking for me so that we can go. Stay still until we are gone so that his dogs do not catch your scent. Here take this." Kimosop was so glad when the young boy whom he had not bothered to ask for his name gave him a plastic bottle with water and two slices of bread."

"That was my lunch. I never finished it. You should move towards that direction. I always hear the sound of vehicles from that side. It is not near but it is worth trying. I have also heard the others say that one has to cross a river before reaching the road. The river is said to be infested with crocodiles." The boy said as he led the goats to the direction the whistle was blowing.

Kimosop waited for about twenty minutes then he started walking. It was now about seven o'clock at night. Fortunately, the moon was shining and he could see where he was stepping. He even saw a snake but it just moved in another direction to avoid him. Back at home Kimosop and the other boys would have picked stones to kill it but Kimosop had no time to waste with a snake which was in its natural environment. A few hours later he saw three animals and his heart sunk. These were not goats. Now he would be eaten alive.

Kimosop hid in a bush to observe the animals and after a short while he concluded that he was not in real danger. They were only giraffes. He had never been close to a giraffe but he knew that they did not eat human beings. However, Kimosop did not dare go near them. The three giraffes had also noticed Kimosop and were curious as they had also never seen a human being so close before. Their sixth sense told them that they were also in no danger hence they decided to investigate their new visitor. Two of the giraffes walked on each side of Kimosop while the third one walked behind him. Kimosop was very frightened. He tried to run but could not do so as it was at night and in the bush. Moreover, each time he was able to increase his speed the giraffes only opened out their steps. Finally he decided to stop

He had never been close to a giraffe but he knew that they did not eat human beings.

and be eaten. After all there was no way out. To his surprise the giraffes also stopped and started to sniff Kimosop as he said his last prayers. He wished Mbaya had found him earlier on and taken him back to the farm. Now he would be sniffed by the giraffes until he died.

"Dear God, you saved me from Mbaya and his dogs, please save me once more. I promise to be a very good boy. Please just tell them to go."

To Kimosop's surprise the giraffes started to walk away. They too had satisfied their curiosity and had decided Kimosop was not edible. Once more Kimosop was out of danger and was grateful to God. This time he took time to kneel down and thank God before he resumed his uncertain journey.

Kimosop walked almost the whole night. He did not dare sleep lest he be eaten by a wild animal. Moreover he did not know whether Mbaya would come to look for him in the morning. So he kept on moving. Some hours later Kimosop came across a footpath and decided to follow it.

"I will just follow it. I don't care where it takes me to, as long as I don't go back to Mbaya's illegal prison," he told himself. It was easier to walk in a foot path than in a forest. Sometimes he even ran. This was a matter of life and death. He would sleep and rest once he got home.

An hour later Kimosop heard another sound and stopped to make sense of it. It was water. He remembered the river that the young boy had told him about. He concluded that the footpath was leading to the river. Two minutes later Kimosop reached the river. There were animal footprints but he could not see any animals. Kimosop walked a few metres along the river bank until he identified a suitable place for crossing the river. There were a few stones he could step on.

"I will take a risk," he said to himself and then looked up to the sky to ask for God's protection.

Kimosop stepped on the first stone, the second and the third but alas this stone moved and shot in the air. It was a crocodile. The starving reptile aimed at Kimosop's leg. He heard a sharp pain in the leg but decided he would not die without a fight. Kimosop was so terrified. The cruel reptile released him but before he could thank God it went for him once more and gripped his shirt. Kimosop gained courage and pulled himself from the reptile which was left with a part of his shirt. He stood and plodded across the river whose water was knee high. He was wet, tired and in pain. He examined himself and noted that he had scratches on the head, arms and legs. His left leg was slightly bleeding but he could still move on.

The incident nearly broke Kimosops heart. He did not know how may other tribulations he was going to face. At one point he even started wondering whether he should stop and wait for Mbaya and his dogs to catch up with him. He however continued walking slowly. Half an hour later he heard another sound which uplifted his spirits. It was the sound of a moving vehicle. He knew that he was near a road. Despite his pains he walked as fast as he could until he reached the road. He was so happy that he started to jump up and down. Finally he would go home. He put his hands in his pocket and found that his money was still there. How nice.

The cruel reptile released him but before he could thank God it went for him once more and gripped his shirt.

"Even if the money is not enough I am sure when the driver of any vehicle hears my story he will not even ask me for money," he told himself.

The sun was already piercing through the sky so Kimosop decided to hide in a bush until he heard a vehicle approach. But Kimosop was so tired and sleepy that he fell deep asleep. He was woken up by the sound of an approaching vehicle but by the time he ran to the road the vehicle was gone. He wanted to cry but he remembered that he was luckier than Masengo and the others who were probably receiving a thorough beating as a result of his escape. Kimosop was now less tired because of the nap he had taken so he decided to stay alert. He waited for a long time until he finally heard the sound of another vehicle. He did not want to wait for another minute.

"I will not miss this one this time," he told himself.

Kimosop ran and stood in the middle of the road. He put up both his arms to make sure that the driver of the vehicle saw him. The driver noticed Kimosop from a distance and was very happy to see his new passenger. He came to a screeching stop. Kimosop was also happy that a vehicle had stopped for him. His story would shock the driver. Kimosop looked up and could not believe his eyes.

"Is this a bad dream or what?" he wondered.

No, this was real. The car in front of him was the small red car with the same man and woman who had abducted him and Tobiko. He fell down and lost consciousness.

CHAPTER 5

FIFTEEN minutes later Kimosop regained consciousness. He found himself sitting at the back seat of the red car.

"Where are you taking me?" he cried but the two people did not bother to speak to him. Kimosop could see outside from the window but could not recognize any of the places they passed. They drove for sometime then the car slowed down.

"Why have you slowed down?" the lady asked the driver.

"There is a Police car ahead. I want to turn back."

"No, if you turn they will be suspicious and follow us. Let us just continue." Then she took out a knife from her pocket and said to Kimosop;

"If you dare make noise or do anything funny I shall cut your throat with this." Kimosop started to cry. Suddenly the car stopped and a police officer came to speak to the driver.

"Good morning. My name is Inspector Komora. My collegues and I are on crime prevention patrols. Where are you going and why did you want to turn around."

"We thought we had lost the way. We are taking my son to the hospital. He was attacked by a crocodile. Look at all the bruises on his body. His clothes are even still wet. He is lucky to be alive," said the lady as Kimosop wondered how she knew that he had been attacked by a crocodile.

"How can you say you are taking him to the hospital and yet you have passed the road leading to the hospital?"

"That is why we wanted to turn back. We realized that we had missed the turn to hospital. Then we saw you and decided to come and confirm the directions to the hospital from you," the lady said.

"Many children have been abducted in this area and we have been directed to check on any child we find in a vehicle. What is your name young boy and why are you crying?"

Kimosop did not say anything. He was too frightened to speak.

"His name is Kimosop. He is my son and is crying because he is in pain," the lady said.

"Kimosop, is this your mother?" Kimosop did not say anything.

"Kimosop, is this your mother?" the policeman asked again.

"Speak Kimosop or I …" the lady shouted.

"Yes, she is my mother," he said.

"Then why are you crying?"

"I was attacked by a crocodile and am very hungry," Kimosop said.

"One final check," said the Inspector as he removed some photographs from his pocket. Kimosop could see the photographs but the lady and the driver could not. The first photograph was Tobiko's. The policeman looked at Kimosop and compared his face with Tobiko's photograph and then put it in his pocket. Then he took out Kones's and Masengo's photographs and many other boys' photographs. Kimosop even saw the photograph of the boy he had met in the forest looking after goats but he dared not say anything.

"Do you know any of these boys?' the policeman asked.

"Yes," said Kimosop.

"When did you last see them," he asked.

"Yesterday," Kimosop responded.

"Kimosop, you did not go to school yesterday you can't have seen them. Why are you lying? Don't you know that a police officer can arrest you for giving false information?" the lady said as she turned around to look at the photographs.

Inspector Komora did not say anything. He just continued looking at different photographs. Then he took out Kimosop's photograph and then looked at Kimosop. Kimosop was so excited but before he could say that it was his photograph the lady said.

"Officer, as you can see my son is injured that is why we are taking him to hospital. Why are you wasting our time yet you can see that this boy is already with his parents?" The lady asked the police officer,

"Do you know any of these boys?' the policeman asked.

"Your son looks like the boy in this photograph," Inspector Komora said pointing at Kimosop's photograph.

"Maybe he looks like him but he is not the one. Children tend to look alike. Please don't keep us any longer or I will raise a complaint against you to your superiors for delaying us despite the fact that my son's injuries are obvious to you," the lady quipped.

The officer thought for a second and then said;

"Ok. You can go. I hope you get well soon Kimosop."

"Thank you officer," the lady said and they drove off.

Thereafter the lady started scolding Kimosop.

"See, you nearly put us into trouble. Why were you crying?"

Kimosop did not say anything. He just kept on crying. He knew that he had lost his only chance to be saved. Now he would face Mbaya and his dogs. They drove up to the house where Kimosop had been staying. The driver honked and immediately Mbaya and the dogs came out.

"I have a pleasant surprise for you. Look in the car," the lady said to Mbaya

"Yes maam," said Mbaya who was very happy to see Kimosop.

"Welcome back, Kimosop. As I told you, if you try to run away you will either be eaten by wild animals or we will catch up with you. Do you believe me now?" He said as he pulled Kimosop out of the car. Kimosop did not even try to resist, he was tired and disheartened. All his efforts had been reduced to naught.

This time Kimosop was locked in a room all by himself. He knew that the other boys were in the same house but he was not allowed to mix with them. He did not know his fate but he knew that he was in big trouble. However, as Kimosop was busy crying something better was also happening elsewhere.

TO begin with Inspector Komora and his collegues were already investigating a rumor that whenever the small red car was seen around one or two children usually disappeared. In addition the children who had been playing in the field with Kones when he ran to get the ball had told the Police that he was pushed into a small red car by a lady. It was also said that the occupants of the small red car had on many occasions tried to offer lifts to other children and when they refused the lady would try to give them sweets or try to force them to enter the car.

Because of such stories police officers suspected the man and the woman who drove in the small red car but did not have enough evidence to arrest them. The Police also feared that if they arrested them without knowing where the children were detained the children could be killed or hurt by other people in the group. So they decided to wait until they were ready.

The other good news was that Inspector Komora had recognized Kimosop as one of the lost boys although Kimosop did not know it. In addition when Kimosop told Inspector Komora that he had seen some of the boys in the pictures 'yesterday' the Inspector believed him and guessed that they must have been locked together. However, the Inspector did not want the man and the woman in the small red car to know that he had recognized Kimosop so as not to put him in danger.

Thereafter as soon Kimosop and his abductors were gone Inspector Komora rushed to the police station and informed his colleagues. They immediately started to prepare themselves so as to rescue the children.

By this time the Police had already discovered that the owners of the small red car lived within the forest reserve. This in itself was a crime as it was illegal for people to live or till the land within the forest reserve. That evening at around six o'clock Inspector Komora and thirty other officers went to the forest reserve accompanied by forest officers. The forest officers knew the area very well because their duties involved guarding the forest against destruction. They divided themselves into three groups and went to different directions.

It was already dark when Inspector Komora and his group approached the house where Kimosop and his collegues were locked. When the lady and the man who usually traveled in the small red car saw car lights they knew that there must be some kind of trouble so they ran and opened for Kimosop to join the other boys. The boys were surprised to see Kimosop as they had thought he was already at his home. They were even shocked that there were other six boys who slept in another house next door.

"Listen. There is no time to talk," the lady said. "But we think the Police are here. You must say that the three of you are my children. Kimosop you are the oldest, followed by you Kones and then Tobiko and these other boys are your friends. If you say anything else I will convince them that you are my children as I did this morning when they saw us with Kimosop. Then you will face this once they are gone," she said as she showed them a gun. The children were really terrified.

A few minutes later Inspector Komora and his group banged the door of the house.

"This house is surrounded. Open the door and put your hands up everybody."

The lady opened the door and recognized Inspector Komora.

"How are you Inspector Komora? We met this morning when I was taking my son to the hospital."

"Where is he?" the inspector asked.

"Kimosop, come out with your brothers and friends," the lady said.

Kimosop, Tobiko and Kones and the others came out with their hands up.

"Put your hands down," the Inspector said. "Now who are you?"

"I told you they are my children and the others are their friends. What else do you want? May be I should call your bosses in Nairobi and tell them how you are harassing me and my family," the lady said but this did not seem to bother the Inspector.

Kimosop, Tobiko and Kones and the others came out with their hands up.

"Is this your mother?" He asked but none of the boys answered.

"My children, confirm to these officers that I am you mother. Go ahead Kimosop," but Kimosop did not utter a word. This time he was not going to make another mistake as had happened in the morning.

Inspector Komora took out some photographs from his pocket. He looked at each boy carefully and gave him his photograph. Then he said;

"Look at the photo you are holding in your hand and if it is not yours give it back to me." None of the boys gave back the photographs.

On seeing this the lady shouted;

"Boys, I am sure you know the consequences."

On hearing this some of the boys became frightened and started to move forward to give back their photographs. Her threats annoyed Inspector Komora who ordered his two constables to handcuff this lady.

"She is not the mother of these children. Arrest the man too."

When the driver of the small red car heard this he tried to escape but was arrested by other officers. The children heard the police officer tell the driver;

"You are under arrest and are not obliged to say anything but whatever you say may be used in evidence."

On hearing this driver kept quiet.

Once the lady and the driver were out of site Inspector Komora asked the boys once more.

"Is that your mother?"

"No," they all said and started to cry as they hugged each other. Each of the boys told Inspector Komora his story. Kones and Tobiko also learnt from Kimosop how he had been caught and brought back.

"And why did you lie to me this morning even after I showed you your picture?" the Inspector asked him.

"She had shown me a knife just before we stopped and said she would kill me if I dared say anything."

"That was wise but I still knew that you were lying. I let her go with you so as not to put the others in danger," the Inspector said.

"And why did you want to surrender your photograph?" Inspector Komora asked the boys.

"She showed us a gun and threatened to use it once you are gone," said Tobiko.

On hearing this, the Inspector ran out and searched the ladies handbag. He found the gun and handed it to one of the officers for safe keeping.

When the operation was over a total of twenty two boys were rescued from the forest reserve. Kimosop was very happy to see the boy who had given him water in the forest. Each group was surprised to know that there were other boys in other parts of the forest.

That evening all the boys were united with their parents, relatives and friends. It was a happy occasion and a big story which was covered in the news media. Kimosop was so happy to be united with his parents. When he got home he took a warm bath and then asked for what he missed most. "Some bread with butter and tea with milk and sugar," he said.

The lady and the man in the red car were taken to court and charged for abduction of the children, child labour, and destruction of the forest since she had constructed a house there illegally. She was also charged with illegal possession of a firearm. It was further noted that her car had false number plates. In total she was jailed for twenty years. The lorry driver was also charged for participating in the abduction.

The most important thing was that Kimosop and all the other children had learnt a lesson. They should never accept a ride or a gift from strangers. Neither should you.

Glossary

abduction	–	taking away of a person against the person's will usually by force
ballast	–	a layer of crushed rock or gravel
blurt	–	to say suddenly without thinking
boast	–	to speak with pride about oneself
butchery	–	a shop for meat
detrimental	–	something that causes harm
diabetes	–	a disease marked by high levels of sugar in the blood
drugged	–	heavily asleep, unconscious, or unable to function after being given drugs
evidence	–	something that makes things plain or clear
infested	–	having large numbers of pests that can cause harm
interrogate	–	to ask questions to a person in order to get answers or information
matatu	–	a public transport vehicle
pillion	–	pad or cushion for another rider behind the main seat or saddle on a horse, motorcycle, bicycle or moped
private	–	something that belongs to a person
rant	–	talk in a wild loud way
siblings	–	children who share parents
tribulations	–	great suffering
vanish	–	to disappear suddenly

www.ingramcontent.com/pod-product-compliance
Lightning Source LLC
Chambersburg PA
CBHW080741180726
48003CB00023B/3292